# THE GATOR GIRLS

# GATOR HALLOWEEN

### by **Stephanie Calmenson**
### and **Joanna Cole**

### illustrated by
### Lynn Munsinger

**Morrow Junior Books**
New York

To Lisa Feierstein

—S.C.


To Danielle and Timmy

—J.C.

Pen-and-ink with watercolor was used for the full-color illustrations.
The text type is 18-point Palatino.

Text copyright © 1999 by Stephanie Calmenson and Joanna Cole
Illustrations copyright © 1999 by Lynn Munsinger

Published by Morrow Junior Books
a division of William Morrow and Company, Inc.
1350 Avenue of the Americas, New York, NY 10019
www.williammorrow.com

Printed in the United States of America.

10  9  8  7  6  5  4  3  2

Library of Congress Cataloging-in-Publication Data
Calmenson, Stephanie.
Gator halloween/by Stephanie Calmenson and Joanna Cole;
illustrated by Lynn Munsinger.
p. cm.
Summary: Amy and Allie, two alligator friends, hope their costumes
will win a prize at the Swamp Street Halloween parade, but they risk missing
the contest to find a lost pet lizard.
ISBN 0-688-14784-4 (trade)—ISBN 0-688-14785-2 (library)
I. Cole, Joanna.   II. Munsinger, Lynn, ill.   III. Title.   PZ7.C136 Gat 1999
[Fic]—dc21   98-44721   CIP AC

# CONTENTS

# 1
# RING...RING...BOO!

*Ring! Ring!* Early Saturday morning the telephone rang at Amy Gator's house.

"I'll get it!" called Amy.

She was sure it was Allie Gator. Allie and Amy were best friends. When they were not together, they were talking on the phone.

"Hello," said Amy.

"Boo!" said a voice at the other end.

"Boo to you, Allie," said Amy.

"Allie whooo?" said the voice. "This is not Allie. This is the ghost next door."

"Ooh, I'm scared," said Amy. "I'm shaking in my shoes."

"Well, I *could* have been a ghost," said the voice, which happened to be Allie's. "It's almost Halloween."

"You're right! And we haven't even thought about our costumes yet," said Amy.

"Meet me downstairs!" said Allie.

"I'm on my way," said Amy.

Allie and Amy both lived on the sixth floor. Their buildings were right next door to each other.

Amy got into her elevator and pushed the first floor button. Allie did the same thing. The elevators went down: *Six, five, four, three, two, one!*

The Gator Girls burst out their doors at the exact same time.

"We need costumes that are special— ones no one else would think of," said Amy.

"You're right," said Allie. "We need a genius plan."

"Let's make costumes that go together," said Amy. "I know! We can be ketchup and mustard."

"Ugh. I hate mustard," said Allie. "How about a pencil and an eraser?"

"Erase that idea," said Amy. "We can do better."

"You're right," said Allie.

The Gator Girls had some thinking to
do. While they thought, they tapped their
tails on the ground. *Tap, tap, tap . . .*

*Whoosh!* A skateboard whizzed by. On
top of the skateboard was an alligator—an
alligator named Marvin.

*Whoosh!* A second skateboard whizzed
by. It was carrying an alligator named
Dave.

"What are you two doing?" Marvin called over his shoulder.

The skateboards circled around and stopped in front of Allie and Amy.

"We heard your tails tapping all the way down the street," said Dave.

"We are thinking," said Amy. "That is something you Gator Guys don't know about."

"If you two are thinking with your tails, you're in big trouble," said Marvin.

"Don't even answer that," said Allie to Amy.

Just then, Gracie came along. Gracie was the Gator Girls' bouncy, bubbly neighbor.

"Hi, everyone," she said, bouncing up and down. "I can't stop now. I'm going to my father's house this week. I'll be back in time for the contest."

"What contest?" asked Allie.

"The costume contest at the Swamp

Street Halloween parade. Speaking of Halloween, here's a spooky joke: What kind of gum do gator ghosts chew?"

The four gators were stumped.

"*Boo*-ble gum!" said Gracie. "Bye! I've got to go!"

After she left, Allie, Amy, Marvin, and Dave sat down. There was going to be a costume contest. They had some thinking to do. *Tap, tap, tap, tap. . .*

# 2
# WHAT COSTUMES?

Suddenly Marvin stood up.

"I've got a great idea for my costume!" he said. "It will be so much fun when I win the prize."

"Or when *I* win it," said Dave. "I've got an idea, too."

The Gator Guys stepped aside and whispered their ideas to each other.

"We'll win the contest together!" said Marvin.

"Right!" said Dave.

Allie and Amy looked at each other. They were not going to take the Gator Guys' bragging sitting down.

"Excuse me," said Allie, jumping up. "I hate to inform you, but the prize is already taken. *We* are going to win the contest."

"The two of you can be the first to congratulate us," said Amy, standing beside Allie.

"No way," said Marvin. "The two of *you* better start practicing your speech. It will begin, 'Congratulations, Marv and Dave.'"

"Not in a gazillion gator years," said Amy. "We're going to win because our costumes will be special—ones no one else would think of."

"You just described our costumes exactly," said Dave.

"Oh, really? Well, we already started making ours, and you should see them," said Allie. "They're prize-winners. Isn't that right, Amy?"

Amy hesitated only a second.

"They sure are!" she said. "They're the best ever!"

"In your dreams," said Marvin. "*Ours* are the best."

"I think it's time to go now," said Allie. "We have to put the finishing touches on our costumes."

"Our *prize-winning* costumes!" said Amy.

The Gator Girls linked arms and stomped off with their noses in the air.

When they were a few feet away, Amy whispered to Allie, "What costumes? We have no idea what we're going to be, do we?"

"Not a clue," Allie whispered back. "Let's go you-know-where."

"To see you-know-who!" said Amy.

The Gator Girls turned the corner and raced wildly toward Madame Lulu's Fortune-Telling Parlor. They needed help from Madame Lulu—fast!

# 3
# MADAME LULU SAYS...

Allie and Amy stood outside Madame Lulu's beaded curtain.

"When I count to three, we'll walk in together," said Allie.

At Madame Lulu's, it felt like Halloween every day of the year. The fortune-telling parlor was pink and yellow outside, but dark and spooky in-side. Allie and Amy were always a little scared to go in.

"One, two, three!" counted Allie.

Neither of them took a step.

*Clink!* The Gator Girls heard a familiar sound. Madame Lulu wore about twenty bracelets on each arm. They clinked together whenever she moved. Allie and Amy could see her shadow through the curtain.

"Enter, fortune-seekers! I've been waiting for you," called the fortune-teller in her husky voice.

Allie and Amy squeezed each other's hands as they walked inside. Madame Lulu was dressed in black. A veil covered her head.

"What brings you here?" she asked, pointing to two chairs.

"W-w-we want our fortunes told, please," said Allie, sliding into one of the chairs.

"We need to know what Halloween costumes we'll wear and if we'll win the contest," said Amy, sliding into the other chair. "Can you help us?"

"Maybe," said the fortune-teller. She held out her hand. *Clink!*

Allie and Amy each dropped a dime into her palm. Madame Lulu slipped the dimes into her pocket. *Clink! Clink!* She gazed into her crystal ball.

"I see darkness. It's darker than usual," she said. "In fact, I can't see a thing."

"Um . . . your veil is covering your eyes," said Allie.

Madame Lulu's veil had slipped down to her chin.

"Ah, yes, you're right," she said. She pushed back the veil. *Clink!*

"That's better," said Madame Lulu. "I see gators in costumes. I see a parade!"

"Wow! That's the Swamp Street Halloween parade," said Amy. She turned to Allie and whispered, "She's amazing!"

"Can you see us? Can you see what we're wearing?" asked Allie.

"It's crowded at the parade," said Madame Lulu.

"Our costumes go together. We're a pair," said Amy.

"Aha! I see a pair of socks!" said Madame Lulu.

"Eewww, smelly! That couldn't be us," said Amy. "Do you see anything else?"

Madame Lulu leaned over and squinted at her crystal ball.

"Sorry. It's growing dark again," she said, holding out her hand. *Clink!* Allie and Amy dropped in two more dimes.

"Much better," said Madame Lulu. "Now I see a baseball and a bat."

"That wouldn't be us. We like soccer," said Allie.

"I see a cup and a saucer," exclaimed Madame Lulu. "Perfect—it's time for my coffee break."

Madame Lulu jumped up.

"But we don't know what our costumes will be!" said Allie.

"Don't worry, you have good ideas all the time. Take a chance! Try your luck! You'll think of something," called Madame Lulu as she headed for the back room.

"We have one last question—will we win the contest?" asked Amy.

"You girls are always winners!" called Madame Lulu over her shoulder.

The next thing they heard was coffee pouring into a cup. Their visit was over. The Gator Girls walked out into the bright sunshine.

"Madame Lulu said we're winners!" cried Amy. "This is so great!"

"Now all we have to do is figure out our costumes," said Allie. "No problem."

# 4
# A WINNING IDEA

The Gator Girls headed to Amy's house for lunch. On the way they saw a sign with a picture of a purple lizard with pink spots. The sign said:

LOST !

Please find Louie

Call 555-FIND

"Ooh, he's so cute!" said Allie.

"I'll bet he's scared," said Amy. "I got lost once, and it was awful."

"Let's try to find him on our way home," said Allie.

The Gator Girls looked high and low. But they didn't spot Louie.

"Maybe his owner found him already," said Allie.

"I hope so," said Amy. "Otherwise Louie's all alone out there."

When they reached Amy's house, her parents had spaghetti with swamp sauce and cheese all ready for them.

"What are you girls doing this afternoon?" asked Amy's father.

"We're making Halloween costumes," said Allie. "Only we can't decide what to be."

"We've been thinking all morning," said Amy.

"Maybe you're thinking too hard," said Amy's mother. "Why don't you do something else? An idea might pop up out of the blue."

"That could work," said Allie.

"Come on," said Amy. "We can play my new board game, Lucky Lizards."

The girls set up the game in Amy's room. They rolled the dice to see who'd go first. Amy got the higher number.

"You're lucky," said Allie.

Amy rubbed the dice in her hands and blew on them.

"Come on, dice, get lucky twice," she said, and tossed them on the board.

"Seven!" said Amy.

She moved seven spaces. The game board read: *Pick a card.*

Amy took a card from the pile. It said, *Take a chance. Roll the dice again.*

"Wow, do you notice something?" said Amy. "The card says *Take a chance.* That's what Madame Lulu told us to do."

"And she said *Try your luck,*" said Allie. "Maybe she was telling us to be a pair of dice."

"That's it! She's a genius!" said Amy.

"So are we!" said Allie. "We figured it out!"

They tapped their tails together.

"Our costumes will be easy to make. We just need cartons and paint," said Allie.

Amy's mother had two cartons in the closet. She helped the girls cut holes for their arms, heads, and tails.

"Now let's go to the art store for the paint," said Amy.

"I can't believe it!" said Allie. "We told Marvin and Dave our costumes were almost finished, and now they really are!"

The Gator Girls got on the elevator. *Six, five, four, three, two, one!* They were on their way.

# 5
# YOU'LL NEVER GUESS

In no time, they were walking in the door of Michael Angelo's Art Store. The lost-lizard poster they'd seen before was hanging on the door.

"Don't forget," said Allie. "We have to look for Louie."

"We will," said Amy.

They stepped up to the counter.

"Hi, Mr. Angelo! We need some black and white paint, please," said Allie.

"We're making our Halloween costumes," said Amy.

"What are you going to be? Penguins?" asked Mr. Angelo.

"No. It's a surprise," said Allie. "You'll see on Halloween."

"Then I'll stop guessing and get the paint," said Mr. Angelo.

He disappeared into the back room.

"Mr. Angelo looks sad today, doesn't he?" said Allie.

"I know. I wonder what's wrong," said Amy.

Just then, the door flew open. Marvin and Dave came in, carrying their skateboards. A moment later, Mr. Angelo came back to the counter with black and white paint for Allie and Amy.

"Hi, Mr. Angelo. We need some red paint," said Marvin. "We're making our Halloween costumes."

"What are you going to be? Apples?" asked Mr. Angelo.

"No," said Dave. "It's a—"

"I know, it's a surprise," said Mr. Angelo. "I'll get your paint."

After he left, Dave turned to Marvin and said, "Look, the goony Gator Girls have black and white paint."

"What are you two going to be? Dalmatians?" asked Marvin.

"No," said Allie.

"Salt and pepper?" said Dave.

"No. You'll never guess our costumes," said Amy.

"You'll never guess ours either," said Dave. "Not in a gazillion gator years."

"We wouldn't spend a gazillionth of a second thinking about it," said Amy.

"Bye, Mr. Angelo," Allie and Amy called on their way out.

"Bye, zebras!" called Marvin.

"We are not going to be zebras," said Allie.

"So long, newspapers!" called Dave.

"We are not going to be newspapers either," said Amy. "You might as well give up. You'll never guess."

And they closed the door behind them.

# 6
# LOOKING
# FOR LOUIE

The Gator Girls hurried back to Amy's
house. They painted the boxes white.

"Okay, let's do the dots now," said
Amy, reaching for the black paint.

"We can't. We have to wait for the white
to dry, or it'll smudge," said Allie.

"What are we going to do while we
wait?" asked Amy.

"I know! Let's look for Louie!" said
Allie.

"Poor Louie! He must be a lonely lizard by now," said Amy.

They ran to the elevator. *Six, five, four, three, two, one!*

The Gator Girls burst out the door.

"I'll go this way. You go that way," said Amy. "We'll have twice as many chances of seeing him."

Amy turned left and started down the street.

"Purple and pink. I need to find purple and pink," she said to herself. "Where would I hide if I were a lizard? I know— I'd hide under something."

As she walked, Amy looked under everything. No lizard. Nothing but ants in sight.

Meanwhile, Allie had headed right.

"If I were a lizard, I'd hide somewhere up high," she said to herself.

Allie looked up at the treetops as she walked. Nothing but squirrels.

*Bam!* Allie and Amy were each turning the corner when they smashed into each other.

"Ouch! Did you find him?" asked Amy.

"Not yet," said Allie, rubbing her head.

"We'll look together," said Amy. "Shout if you see anything purple and pink."

They headed up Swamp Street. They saw a red bird, a yellow flower, and an orange pumpkin.

"I see purple and pink!" said Amy, running ahead.

"Is it Louie?" asked Allie, racing to catch up.

"Nope. It's a flowerpot," said Amy. "But at least it's the right colors."

"It's time for a break," said Allie. "I bet our costumes are dry."

The Gator Girls went back to Amy's house and painted black dots on their dice.

"Now we have to wait again," said Allie. "I'm hungry."

"Okay, let's go to the kitchen. We have to roll if we're going to be dice," said Amy.

They started to do somersaults.

"Stop! We won't be able to roll like this on Halloween. We'll be wearing boxes," said Allie.

"Then we'll have to do cartwheels," said Amy.

"Good idea," said Allie. "One, two, three, go!"

They cartwheeled into the kitchen. Amy's father was making popcorn.

"Bravo!" he said when they landed at the table. "How are your costumes?"

"Excellent! Perfect! Wonderful!" said Allie.

"Wet," said Amy.

"Here, have some popcorn. It's dry," said Amy's father, kidding around.

By the time the bowl was empty, the costumes were ready for Halloween. The Gator Girls were, too.

45

# 7
# WE CAN'T BE LATE!

All week long, Allie and Amy looked for Louie.

They saw lots of purple and pink things. But they didn't see a purple-and-pink lizard.

*Ding, dong!* On Halloween, the doorbell rang at Amy's house.

"Trick-or-treaters already?" said Amy's mother, opening the door.

"No, it's me!" said Allie as she walked in. "Amy and I have to hurry. We can't be late for the parade!"

The Gator Girls put on their costumes. Amy wore a white bow and white shoes. Allie wore black. They stood in front of the mirror.

There were four dots on the front of Allie's costume and six dots on Amy's.

"Four plus six equal . . . ," said Amy.

"A perfect ten!" said Allie. "We're the best."

"And we are right on time," said Amy. "Let's go."

The Gator Girls walked down Swamp Street and turned onto Everglade Avenue. Everywhere they looked, they saw great costumes.

"I love Halloween!" said Amy.

"And we're going to win the contest!" said Allie. "Madame Lulu said so."

"She's never been wrong yet," said Amy.

Suddenly, the Gator Girls stopped.

"Do you see what I see?" asked Allie, looking down a side street.

"You mean the purple-and-pink nose

sticking out of that crack in the wall?" said Amy.

"It's Louie! Let's get him," said Allie.

"But we'll be late for the parade," said Amy. "We can come back for him later."

"He might be gone by then," said Allie.

"You're right. We can't leave him. If he were my pet, I'd want someone to rescue him," said Amy. "Let's go!"

As soon as they got near, the nose disappeared farther into the wall.

"Uh-oh," said Amy.

She ran and got a leaf. "Maybe he'd like something to eat," she said.

Amy dangled the leaf in front of the crack.

"He's not moving," said Allie. "Getting him out will take forever. We'll miss the contest."

"We've got to do something," said Amy. "He needs our help."

"Come out, Louie!" called Allie.

As soon as she called him, the lizard inched forward.

"Wow! He knows his name!" said Amy.

"Here, Louie!" called Allie and Amy together. "Louie! Louie! Come out!"

Inch by inch, Louie crept out.

"One more baby lizard step, Louie," said Amy.

"He looks just like his picture," said Allie.

Louie walked out and climbed up on Amy's head.

"Look where he is!" said Amy, trying not to move.

She rolled her eyes up and looked at Louie. Louie looked down.

"I'm in love!" said Amy.

"I want him to climb on me!" said Allie.
Just then, Louie took a giant leap. He
landed on Allie's shoulder.

"Way to go, Louie!" said Allie.
"Uh-oh," said Amy, looking at her
watch. "We *really* have to go now!"

"But what about Louie?" asked Allie.

"We'll bring him along," said Amy. "Louie, you're invited to a parade!"

# 8
# CONGRATULATIONS, YOU WON!

"We're so lucky," said Amy. "We found Louie."

He was now on Amy's shoulder.

"And we're going to win the contest, too," said Allie, gently patting Louie's tail.

The Gator Girls looked up ahead. A witch with a tall black hat and a broom was standing on a platform. A ghost and a goblin holding prizes were next to her.

All around the platform were paraders in costumes.

"And now for our first prize. The winner is . . . the basketball!" said the witch.

"The winner? We missed the contest!" said Amy.

Everyone started to clap as the basketball bounced up to the platform.

"That basketball's so bouncy, it's got to be Gracie!" said Allie.

The witch handed a shiny jack-o'-lantern statue to the basketball.

"Congratulations, you won!" she said.
*Clink! Clink!*

"Did you hear those bracelets?" said Allie. "The witch is Madame Lulu!"

Then they heard the basketball ask, "Do you want to hear a Halloween joke? What do you call Jack-o'-Lantern's sister?"

"I give up," said Madame Lulu.

"Jill-o'-Lantern!" said the basketball.

"That's *definitely* Gracie," said Amy.

"How can she be the winner? Madame Lulu said *we're* winners," said Allie.

*Clang! Clang!* A red fire engine whizzed into view.

"We're here!" said the front of the fire engine.

"You can give us our prize now," said the back of the fire engine.

"Marvin? Dave? Is that you?" asked Allie.

"Absolutely not," said both ends of the fire engine.

"Well, you're *absolutely* late," said Amy. "Gracie just won the contest."

Suddenly an excited voice called out from the crowd, "Louie! It's my Louie!"

Marvin and Dave's heads popped up from the fire truck as everyone turned to see who the voice belonged to.

# 9
# TRICK OR TREAT!

The voice belonged to Mr. Angelo. He picked up his lizard and hugged him.

"I missed you so much, Louie," he said.

"He's *your* pet lizard?" said Amy to Mr. Angelo.

"No wonder you looked so sad," said Allie.

Louie settled happily on Mr. Angelo's shoulder.

"How did you find him? It couldn't have been easy," said Mr. Angelo.

"Well, it took awhile. That's why we were late," said Allie.

"That means you missed the contest. For Louie. And for me!" said Mr. Angelo.

"It was worth it," said Amy.

"We love Louie. We're going to miss him," said Allie.

"You can come visit," said Mr. Angelo. "I get very busy at the store, and I think he gets lonely."

"We would love to visit!" said Allie. "We could feed him."

"And take him for walks," said Amy.

"I would like to reward you somehow," said Mr. Angelo. "I know! How would you like drawing lessons?"

"That would be so great!" said Allie. "Louie could be our model. And the lessons will be our prize."

"Madame Lulu *said* we're winners!" said Amy.

"And she's never been wrong yet," said Allie.

• • •

*Ding-dong!* Later that night, the doorbell rang at Madame Lulu's Fortune-Telling Parlor. The sun was going down, and it was starting to feel just a little bit spooky outside.

"Who is it?" called Madame Lulu.

She pushed aside the beaded curtain. Standing in front of her were a pair of dice, a red fire engine, and a basketball.

"Trick or treat!" called five voices.

Madame Lulu dropped treats in everyone's Halloween bags.

"Don't go away," she said.

She brought out her crystal ball.

"Ooh, we're going to get our fortunes told!" said Allie.

"What do you see?" asked Marvin.

"Are there any tricks?" asked Amy.

Madame Lulu gazed into her ball.

"There will be no tricks tonight—only treats," she said. "Happy Halloween!"

Then the fire engine clanged. The basketball bounced. And the dice tapped their tails together as they cartwheeled down the street.